THIS S
BELON

_____

I THINK MY CAT IS A SPY!

by Rayla Ray

Ever since we brought
home our Kitty,

something's been a little fishy...

While Kitty may appear to be a simple household cat,

I don't think normal cats are supposed to act like that!

I can't seem to figure Kitty
out even though I try.

That's why I think
my cat is a spy!

Sometimes, Kitty lies on the couch and takes up a lot of space.

But when I turn around, I see Kitty has disappeared without a trace!

I look and look but can't find
Kitty anywhere.

Then I realize that Kitty has just been sitting in that chair!

Out of everyone I know, Kitty has the best eye sight.

She must have night vision goggles that help her see at night!

When I hug Kitty, she tries to escape with the utmost urgency.

I think Kitty just wants to stay prepared in case there is a spy emergency!

Kitty reeeeaaalllly hates getting her nails cut.

I'm guessing she needs them
to kick her enemy's butt!

Kitty could fall from great heights and still land gracefully.

They must teach that kind of thing at the Kitty Spy Academy!

I often find Kitty staring blankly at the air.

I don't understand what she's looking at, because there is never anything there!

At night, Kitty starts to run
around endlessly...

She must need the practice if she ever wants to catch a really fast spy enemy!

When I pet Kitty, she starts to vibrate and purr intensely.

What if she's sending a signal against a potential enemy?

**Kitty loves chasing things
and she's great at hunting…**

Kitty likes to have lots of staring contests with me.

I wonder if Kitty is trying to tell me something telepathically...

Whether a space is wide or tight,
Kitty always fits in.

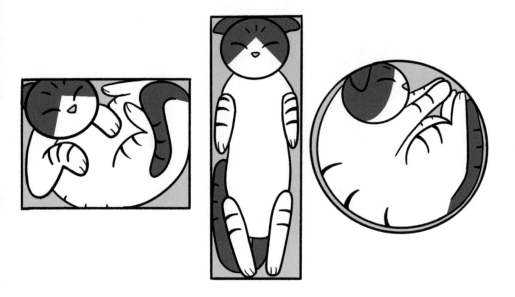

It's like she can shape shift from
big and fat to small and thin!

I find Kitty sleeping
even when the sky
is bright.

I guess spy cats do most of
their work late at night...

Kitty hates water and
never joins me in the pool.

I guess they never taught Kitty how to swim in spy school...

When I confront Kitty about being a spy, she acts all dumb and shy.

She won't reveal her
secrets no matter
how hard I try!

But Kitty does too many things which I can't explain why...

And that's why I think my cat is a spy!

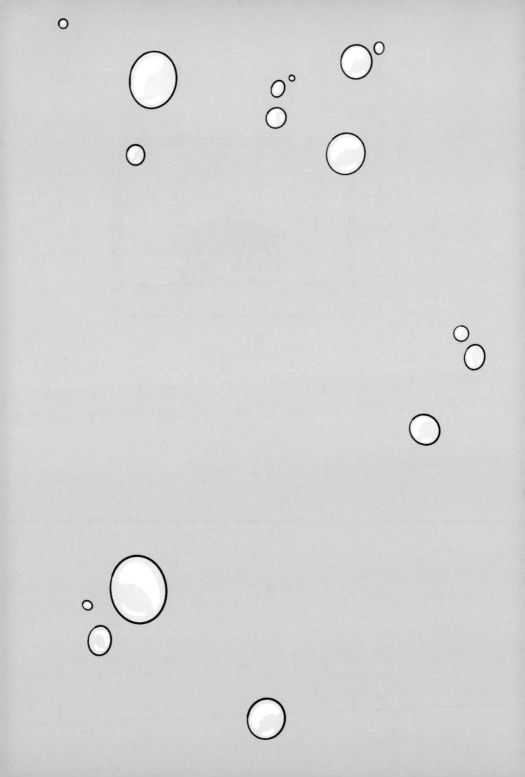

PSSSSSSST!

HEY, YOU!
YES, YOU!

DID YOU LIKE
THIS BOOK?

ARE YOU
CONVINCED MY
CAT IS A SPY?!

IS *YOUR* CAT
A SPY TOO?

LET ME KNOW ON THE NEXT PAGE!

I WOULD LOVE TO HEAR FROM YOU! IF YOU ENJOYED THIS BOOK, PLEASE LET ME KNOW BY LEAVING A REVIEW IN THE LINK BELOW! YOUR SUPPORT MEANS I CAN CONTINUE TO MAKE BOOKS AND YOU CAN CONTINUE TO ENJOY THEM. PLUS IT JUST MEANS A LOT. LIKE EMOTIONALLY.

THANK YOU!

Made in United States
Troutdale, OR
07/13/2023

11202896R00026